Illustrated by Katherine Lawless

Copyright © 1998 Modern Publishing, a division of Unisystems, Inc.
Previously published as ™Fun-To-Read Fairy Tales.
All rights reserved.
® Honey Bear Books is a trademark owned by Honey Bear Productions, Inc.,
and is registered in the U.S. Patent and Trademark Office. No part of this book may be
reproduced or copied in any format without written permission from the publisher.
All rights reserved. Printed in China.

2 4 6 8 10 9 7 5 3 1

CHRISTMAS CLASSICS
The Twelve Days of Christmas

MODERN PUBLISHING
A Division of Unisystems, Inc.
New York, New York 10022
Series UPC Number: 39495

On the first day of Christmas,
My true love gave to me
A partridge in a pear tree.

On the second day of Christmas,
My true love gave to me
Two turtledoves
And a partridge in a pear tree.

On the third day of Christmas,
My true love gave to me
Three French hens,
Two turtledoves
And a partridge in a pear tree.

On the fourth day of Christmas,
My true love gave to me
Four calling birds,
Three French hens,
Two turtledoves
And a partridge in a pear tree.

On the fifth day of Christmas,
My true love gave to me
Five gold rings;
Four calling birds,
Three French hens,
Two turtledoves
And a partridge in a pear tree.

On the sixth day of Christmas,
My true love gave to me
Six geese a-laying,
Five gold rings;
Four calling birds,
Three French hens,
Two turtledoves
And a partridge in a pear tree.

On the seventh day of Christmas,
My true love gave to me
Seven swans a-swimming,
Six geese a-laying,
Five gold rings;
Four calling birds,
Three French hens,
Two turtledoves
And a partridge in a pear tree.

On the eighth day of Christmas,
My true love gave to me
Eight maids a-milking,
Seven swans a-swimming,
Six geese a-laying,

Five gold rings;
Four calling birds,
Three French hens,
Two turtledoves
And a partridge in a pear tree.

On the ninth day of Christmas,
My true love gave to me
Nine ladies dancing,
Eight maids a-milking,
Seven swans a-swimming,
Six geese a-laying,
Five gold rings;
Four calling birds,
Three French hens,
Two turtledoves
And a partridge in a pear tree.

On the tenth day of Christmas,
My true love gave to me
Ten lords a-leaping,
Nine ladies dancing,
Eight maids a-milking,
Seven swans a-swimming,
Six geese a-laying,
Five gold rings;
Four calling birds,
Three French hens,
Two turtledoves
And a partridge in a pear tree.

On the eleventh day of Christmas,
My true love gave to me
Eleven pipers piping,
Ten lords a-leaping,
Nine ladies dancing,
Eight maids a-milking,
Seven swans a-swimming,
Six geese a-laying,
Five gold rings;
Four calling birds,
Three French hens,
Two turtledoves
And a partridge in a pear tree.

On the twelfth day of Christmas,
My true love gave to me
Twelve drummers drumming,

Eleven pipers piping,
Ten lords a-leaping,

Nine ladies dancing,
Eight maids a-milking,
Seven swans a-swimming,
Six geese a-laying,

Five gold rings;
Four calling birds,
Three French hens,
Two turtledoves

And a partridge in a pear tree!